Grover's Mommy

By Liza Alexander
Illustrated by
David Prebenna

Featuring Jim Henson's Sesame Street Muppets

A GOLDEN BOOK • NEW YORK

Published by Golden Books Publishing Company, Inc.,
in conjunction with Children's Television Workshop

A portion of the money you pay for this book goes to Children's Television Workshop.
It is put right back into SESAME STREET and other CTW educational projects. Thanks for helping!

Library of Congress Catalog Card Number: 93-78489 ISBN: 0-307-30203-2   MCMXCVII

Say hello to someone really special.
Say hello to Grover's mommy!

Do you want to know what Grover's mommy does?

Well, she is an excellent painter.

And she is a terrific chef.

Grover's mommy is a real daredevil.

And she is a mechanical genius.

Grover's mommy is a math whiz.

And she is an amazing magician.

Grover's mommy is a brilliant doctor.

And she is a fearless explorer.

Grover's mommy is a marvelous farmer.

And she is an expert costume designer.

Grover's mommy is a Super mommy!